GLADIATOR BOY

RESCUE MISSION

Other Gladiator Boy titles to collect:

GLADIATOR BOY

RESCUE MISSION

DAVID GRIMSTONE

Hodder
Children's
Books

A division of Hachette Children's Books

Text copyright © 2009 David Grimstone
Illustration copyright © 2009 James de la Rue

First published in Great Britain in 2009
by Hodder Children's Books

The rights of David Grimstone to be identified as the author
and James de la Rue to be identified as the illustrator of the Work have been
asserted by them in accordance with the Copyright, Designs and Patents Act 1988.

I

ISBN: 978 0 340 98910 4

Typeset by Tony Fleetwood

Printed in the UK by CPI Bookmarque, Croydon, CR0 4TD

The paper and board used in this paperback by Hodder Children's Books
are natural recyclable products made from wood grown in sustainable
forests. The manufacturing processes conform to the
environmental regulations of the country of origin.

Hodder Children's Books
a division of Hachette Children's Books
338 Euston Road, London NW1 3BH
An Hachette UK company

www.hachette.co.uk

For Barbara Ann Stone, my mother.

I would like to dedicate the entire Gladiator Boy *series to Terry Pratchett. There is no writer, living or dead, for whom I have greater respect. Thank you for everything.*

CONTENTS

ANCIENT ITALY

PREVIOUSLY IN GLADIATOR BOY

Decimus Rex is recaptured by Slavious Doom following a determined assault on Suvius Tower. However, with one friend dead and the others in terrible danger, Decimus soon learns the price he must pay for his bold defiance of the grim overlord . . .

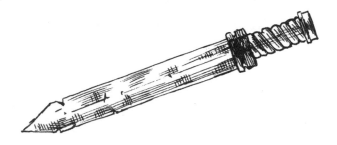

CHAPTER
I

THE
PROPHECY

Decimus Rex had been confined in a small cell for six days. It wasn't any old cell, he realized upon entering, but the same dusty room he had occupied during the trials. The trials now seemed so far in the past that they almost felt like stories he'd heard from someone else. However, there was one major difference this time: the rest of the cell block was empty.

Decimus hadn't seen Olu, Ruma, Argon or Gladius since they'd been captured in the courtyard of Suvius Tower. At first, he'd fully expected the group to be separated. They were obviously stronger together, and the simple fact that Doom had used the others as a trap to capture him and Olu meant that they were valuable to him. At least, that is the story Decimus told himself: Doom could have killed them all at the tower had he wished to see them dead.

Still, Decimus was here in this pitiful cell and they were not. His mind raced back to the scene in the courtyard, as he tried to think past the death of Teo and focus on the things Doom had told him as he stood over the dark master's dead assassin.

He was special. Decimus didn't see how or why, and he'd certainly never felt that special, growing up in Tarentum. Nevertheless, Doom had told him that he had a destiny and that destiny had something to do with a task Decimus needed to complete, a task only he could achieve and one that Doom was desperate for him to undertake. So, as the evil overlord had explained in a mocking voice, his friends would be used as bargaining chips . . . but if so, where were they all?

Decimus huddled in the corner of the cell and awaited his fate. Food was being brought to him three times a day, along with a large jug of water which saw him through the night. They were treating him well: he doubted the same was true for his friends.

The first four days had passed in a blur, but the last two had lingered . . . and now Decimus felt himself yearning for light and fresh air, even if it meant leaping spikes and running across burning coals. He slept badly.

On the seventh night, however, two burly guards marched into the passage and unlocked the door to his cell.

'Out.'

It wasn't a suggestion, and Decimus found himself hauled off his feet even as he tried to sit up. The gruff pair shoved him against the wall in the outer corridor and stalked him like two savage lions tracking a wounded gazelle. Decimus walked along the passage, glancing back every few moments to check that he was going in the right direction. They passed several junctions and came to the foot of a long flight of steps. Looking up into the torchlit gloom, Decimus suddenly knew where he was going – he took a deep breath, and prepared himself for the worst.

Slavious Doom wasn't sitting on the golden throne he usually occupied when receiving visitors. Instead, he stood beside a vast table that was literally weighed down with scrolls, folded parchments and several heavy stones that were being used to keep the largest of the scrolls spread open.

Doom turned as Decimus half-walked and half-stumbled into the room. The two guards didn't follow the young slave inside, but slammed the great double doors behind him instead.

A grim silence settled over the room, but it was shattered quickly.

'What have you done with my friends?' Decimus snapped. 'I'll do whatever you want if you let them go.'

A sudden, maniacal laughter filled the room, and Slavious Doom turned slowly to face his young guest. A sick smile had spread across his thick lips and, as he stepped forward, Decimus was reminded of the overlord's immense size; the man was a giant, plain and simple.

'To the best of my knowledge, your friends are all alive . . . though I doubt they are enjoying themselves.' Doom pointed a finger at the slave and his smile suddenly became a demonic grin. 'Nevertheless, young Decimus, I will NOT release your friends and you WILL complete the task that is your destiny. You have no choice in the matter – I have seen to that.'

Decimus felt a whirlwind of anger rise up

inside him. He balled his hands into fists, squeezing them so tightly that his knuckles turned white.

Doom, however, stepped back from the boy and leant upon the nearest edge of the scroll-covered table.

'You have a mark on your neck,' he said, simply. 'An elongated cross. You have had it since you were born, and your parents probably think nothing of it. I doubt you even know it exis—'

'I know,' Decimus barked. 'It's just a birthmark; what of it?'

Doom glanced down at the scrolls beside him before returning his attention to the slave.

'The mark is, in fact, a sword, and one that truly exists: a blade of legend that is said to glow with unearthly flame. That sword lies deep in a maze of catacombs beneath this arena. I have been trying to retrieve it for many years and I have lost . . . countless servants in the process. No one survived, for the catacombs are crowded with perils, and each one offers nothing but grizzly death for all who enter.' He released a heavy sigh. 'I ignored the prophecies, you see, the ones you will see scrawled on the walls as you enter – the prophecies that tell of a certain boy born with a certain mark . . . a boy destined to retrieve the sword. A boy, Decimus, just like you.' Doom smiled again, his eyes alight with a hungry excitement. 'We found you purely by chance – one of my guards noticed the mark when you were captured. What luck! Hahahah!'

For a moment, the young slave was speechless. Then he felt the anger boil inside him once again.

'NO,' he growled, the words leaving his mouth in a grumble but echoing in the chamber like thunder.

Doom raised one dark eyebrow.

'No? Hmm . . . by that I must take it that you are refusing my request?'

'I will not go into the dungeon and I will NOT retrieve the sword – until I know that my friends are safe.'

Slavious Doom practically exploded with laughter. One giant hand clapped over his jaw and his shoulders shook with the effort required to hold in the mirth.

'You will go forth and seek out the sword, my young friend, for one simple reason, and one only. I have sent your friends into the catacombs ahead of you.'

As Doom's booming voice erupted into sardonic laughter, Decimus found himself frozen to the spot with fear. It was true, he knew so immediately: the evil warlord had found a way to make him cooperate. Argon, Gladius, Ruma and Olu were all somewhere far below the arena . . . and they needed his help.

CHAPTER
II

THE

MAP

The following morning, when Decimus emerged from the shadowy depths of the arena and stepped into the brilliant sunshine, a crowd of slaves, servants and training masters had gathered on the sands. He immediately recognized Truli, the jailer who had patrolled his cell block during the trials, and – half hidden at the back of the throng – Mori and Falni, two of the three trial-masters who had put him and his friends through the rigorous elimination contests.

At the front of the group stood Slavious Doom, exuding an aura of fear that seemed to keep even his own bodyguards at a generous distance.

Decimus didn't flinch, bow his head or

take any sort of backward step from the arena overlord. Instead, he stared directly into Doom's eyes.

'Well?' he snapped. 'Where's the entrance to this hell-hole?'

A collective gasp went up from the crowd, but Doom strode forward and thrust a parchment into the young slave's unresisting hand.

'The entrance is behind you, beyond the iron door. You may wish to study this first, however.'

Decimus unfurled the parchment, which was almost entirely blank apart from a small collection of hastily scrawled lines in one corner. He thought he recognized the scroll as the one that had been pinned to the table in

Doom's lavish quarters.

'What's this supposed to be?' he asked, turning it over in his hands.

'It is a map,' said Doom, quietly. 'A map drawn by the only person ever to successfully enter the catacombs and survive.'

Decimus studied the lines in the corner of the parchment. 'I thought you said no one had ever survived,' he muttered. 'Besides, there are only four or five tunnels on this map . . .'

Doom nodded. 'That's because I . . . well . . .' The overlord grimaced, his expression hollow. 'That map is of my making, and I was unable to proceed any further due to a . . . surprise attack.'

Decimus locked eyes with the warlord

once again. 'It's utterly pathetic,' he growled. 'You couldn't cope in this place yourself, yet you sent my friends into the tunnels so I would have to go in for you.' He returned his gaze to the map, aware that the entire crowd had taken several steps back following his verbal assault on their master. 'You know something, Doom? I bet Olu, Argon and Ruma are already further inside the catacombs than this. I bet even Gladius could fill this map i—'

Without warning, Doom charged the young slave and barrelled into him, sending Decimus flying backwards. The sand exploded around him as he landed in a crumpled heap, the map flying from his hands in the process.

Roaring with anger at the slave's insult, Doom leapt into the air and threw his entire body forward, landing with an armoured elbow outstretched . . .

. . . but Decimus wasn't there.

Rising to his feet with near-lightning

speed, the young slave dived

sideways and rolled in the sand several

times, coiling like a serpent before

springing back on to his toes.

Doom clambered up, himself, but he was slow in comparison. All around him, his servants stepped forward and then back, each eager to assist their master but aware that they might be punished for rescuing him from a mere child.

Doom's next charge at Decimus was an even bigger disaster. A fist swung with incredible energy missed its mark, as did a kick which would probably have broken the young slave's leg in half.

Decimus, determined to put on a show for Doom's 'select' crowd, snaked around the giant warlord's blows, delivering one of his own to the side of Doom's bulbous neck. Then, just as the big man drove a knee

towards him, Decimus deftly leapt back and,
grabbing a handful of sand, blinded his
opponent with a fine mist.

This last move was too much for the trial-
masters, who quickly dashed forward and
seized Decimus by the arms. Dragging the
young slave off his feet, the two masters
began to deliver a rain of blows to his back
and shoulders. Suddenly, however, a loud
voice erupted around them.

'STOP!' screamed Doom,
clambering to his feet
and frantically
rubbing his
eyes. 'He must
not be harmed!'

Mori and

Falni quickly released Decimus, and both leapt away from him as if he'd just turned into a rampaging tiger.

Almost shaking with rage, Doom stomped across the arena floor and, snatching up the map, brought his head to within an inch of Decimus's steely glare.

'You can discover what evil prowls those tunnels, yourself: the hard way. I was going to offer you the map, weapons and armour to assist your passage through the catacombs, but why should I bother? After all, if you are the chosen one, you will need no weapons. Ha! There is only one way in and out of the depths . . . so you have no choice but to return to me . . . and if you return without that sword, I will kill your friends right in front of you. Good luck, you little wretch.'

He turned and strode back to the nervous crowd, waving an arm behind him.

'Behold the mighty Decimus Rex, chosen among many to seek the Blade of Fire and return it to its rightful owner: Slavious Doom!'

'Doom!'

'Doom!'

'Doom!'

The crowd boomed the name as though they were engaged in a collective chant, stamping their feet and, in some cases, their shields on the arena floor.

Decimus muttered under his breath and, turning on his heels, marched straight past the iron door and proceeded along the darkened corridor beyond.

After a short walk, he came to the end of the tunnel and was surprised to find five large and muscular guards standing sentry beside a thick iron pole that seemed to be wedged between the floor and ceiling of the corridor. Decimus noted that it was covered in thick chains, and that each chain was held

loosely by one of the guards. Beneath the pole, set into the floor of the passage, was a smooth iron plate.

As Decimus approached, the guards began to heave on the chains, all pulling in the same direction. At length, after much grunting and groaning, the pole began to shift, great swathes of cavern dust drifting down from the ceiling as it moved. It literally took all five of the brutes to shift the pole and, once it had been removed, the plate itself required three sets of arms in order to lift it.

The guards holding the burden staggered to the end of the passage and eventually managed to lean it on one side against the wall. The other two were still supporting the pole between them.

For the first time since the battle at Suvius Tower, Decimus felt suddenly afraid. Evidently, there was something in the catacombs below that was capable of bursting through an iron plate that three enormous men could barely lift: only the wedged iron pole could keep it down there.

Determined to show no outward signs of the terror he was feeling inside, Decimus simply walked up to the hole in the floor and crouched down beside it.

'Am I supposed to jump?' he said, squinting in an effort to see to the bottom of the hole.

'Take this,' muttered one of the guards, handing him a thick length of rope. 'Lower yourself down.'

Decimus allowed his eyes to follow the

rope to its source, an iron ring protruding from the passage wall. He swallowed a few times, took hold of the rope and let his legs dangle into the hole.

Don't think, he told himself. Just do it.

Decimus took one last glance at the guards, then lowered himself down into the darkness.

CHAPTER III

THE CATACOMBS

Decimus wriggled off the end of the rope and dropped on to what felt like a pile of rubble, staggering slightly as his feet scrambled for a grip in the dark. He threw out his arms to maintain some sort of balance, but the gesture actually tipped him over and he tumbled backwards, landing awkwardly on the rock-pile.

Gazing up towards the hole in the roof of the cave, Decimus saw the distant flicker of torchlight. Starting as a tiny ball of flame, the light grew bigger and bigger until he realized what was happening and quickly wriggled out of the way. The torch landed on the rock-pile, still burning brightly, and immediately illuminated the cave he was standing in. The darkness fled.

Decimus snatched the torch from the rubble, and was about to shout some sort of acknowledgement to the guards when he saw the iron plate suddenly drop over the gap, sealing him inside the catacombs. Evidently,

the arena guards weren't taking any chances.

Decimus gulped a lungful of the fetid air and, raising the torch high over his head, began to look around him.

The cave was more of a cavern, and there seemed to be several exits. Decimus lowered the torch to the ground, but there were no obvious footprints. He would have to work out some other way of tracking down the others. At first he felt sure they would have stuck together and taken one passage, but then another thought occurred: what if they had been sent into the catacombs separately, one at a time? It seemed the cruel and spiteful thing to do, and Slavious Doom was nothing if not cruel.

Decimus raised the torch once again, and

slowly turned in a circle, studying each of the

passageways that snaked off from the

entrance cave: they all looked similar and

none stood out as an obvious choice. There

was no noise, either – the place seemed eerily quiet. He was beginning to wish he'd kept hold of Doom's pitiful map.

So . . . there were eight tunnels.

It would help, Decimus thought, if he knew how long ago the others had been sent down here. After all, they could have anything up to a six day lead on him . . .

The image of Gladius impaled on a spike in some subterranean chamber crept into his mind, but he managed to fight off the thought before it became too vivid to put aside.

Just choose one, he told himself, and follow it through. They're probably all connected.

Holding aloft the flaming torch, Decimus

headed along the nearest tunnel, ducking slightly when it became apparent that the passage sloped sharply downwards. For a time, it seemed as though the ground might actually collapse beneath his feet, and he cursed himself for making a bad choice . . . but the uneven floor soon gave way to sludge and he found himself squelching steadily downwards.

He'd been moving in the same direction for what seemed like an age when the corridor suddenly opened out and a curious sight greeted him.

The passage beyond was flooded, and looked more like a functioning sewer than a long-forgotten tunnel network. The water was a dirty green colour, and indeed the entire corridor seemed to be bathed in an emerald glow: Decimus couldn't tell whether this was something to do with the reflection of his own torchlight or another source of illumination that he couldn't yet see.

Still, at least one thing was certain: the only way onward was through the green river ... and that meant either wading or, if the water was deep, swimming the channel, a murky creek that could be teeming with ... well, with anything.

Decimus took another gulp of the stale air and moved, slowly and very carefully, into the water. It was cold and filthy, and he stirred up a great deal of floating debris as he progressed. Already up to his waist, Decimus suddenly realized how stupid he had been to

head for the middle of the tunnel and quickly
moved to the left side instead. There, he
could grip the wall with one hand while
holding the torch above the water with the
other. That way, even if the water was more
than twice his own height, he could still
support himself above the surface . . . which
was just as well.

One more step and Decimus went straight
down, so surprised by the sudden dip that he
just managed to snatch hold of the wall

before he was completely submerged. The torch slipped dangerously close to the water, and one corner of it brushed the surface and went out. Decimus reacted quickly, thrusting his right hand upward so as not to lose more of the flame. His fingers were digging into the wall so fiercely that he actually needed to grit his teeth and summon a great effort to push himself forward and release them. He floated for a mere half-second before grabbing the wall once again, propelling himself forward using what strength he could muster.

It was at this point that Decimus first noticed the end of the tunnel . . . and the crocodile that was slowly crawling down the far bank towards the water. A sudden panic gripped him, and he flinched at the sight, dropping his torch in the process. The flames went out: suddenly, the entire corridor was plunged into shadow, only a pale glow from the passage beyond giving any illumination to the flooded chamber.

Decimus heard a loud splash . . . and the nightmare began.

CHAPTER
IV

THE
CRY

Decimus knew very little about crocodiles. He'd only seen one in his entire life: it was kept as a pet by a merchant in Tarentum. He remembered the creature partly due to its terrifying appearance and partly because it ended up devouring the merchant when he slipped into the feeding pool one morning. According to one witness, he'd been dangling a fish over the water and attempting to hold a conversation with his wife at the same time. The beast had snatched hold of his arm and dragged him in. A single scrap of robe was the only item reclaimed from the pool.

Decimus took a deep breath, and tried desperately to think straight. He was approximately halfway along the tunnel, so it would be no good trying to swim back: the crocodile was already spearing through the water with amazing speed and would easily catch up with him. Squinting up at the shadowy ceiling, Decimus suddenly glimpsed his only hope of avoiding the jaws of the beast . . . and it was a slim hope, at best. Digging his fingers into the cracks in the tunnel wall, he began to scramble upwards, feeling for gaps with his toes at the same time. Finding one that was almost at chest height, he drove his foot into the crevice and forced his entire body out of the water. The crocodile was now nothing more than a ripple in the water, but Decimus knew it was closing in on him, fast.

Wedging his feet in the crooked wall

space, he freed one hand in order to feel further along the curved ceiling of the tunnel. The search revealed a single gap, larger than the one he'd found previously, but there was no second space for his feet. If he managed to take hold of the larger gap, he would end up hanging from the roof of the tunnel.

Decimus groaned in the shadows; the

crocodile was almost upon him. Half reaching, half scrambling, he drove his outstretched hand into the gap and swung his legs in a wild arc . . . just as the crocodile erupted from the water and snapped its incredible jaws in the space he had occupied a mere instant before.

Crying out with the effort of strength the manoeuvre required, he tucked his legs

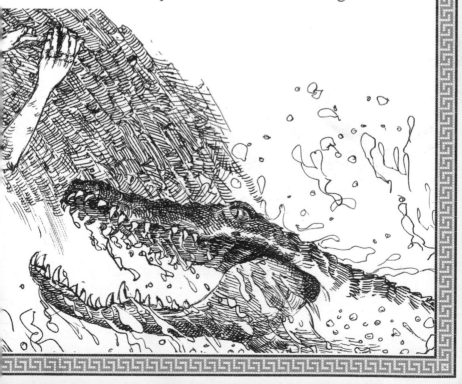

under him and worked his other hand into the gap, pulling himself as close to the roof of the tunnel as he could manage. He gasped: every muscle in his body felt stretched to breaking point, and a line of sweat glistened on his forehead.

Below him, the crocodile reared up again, but this time there was a sizeable gap between his feet and the snap of its jaws.

The great reptile splashed back beneath the water and circled round again, obviously preparing to attack from a different position.

'Arghhghgh!'

The scream erupted from his throat before he knew it was happening, and took him completely by surprise. The pain in his arms was now almost unbearable and, judging by

the lack of crevices in the tunnel roof, the situation wasn't about to get any better. Decimus knew, instinctively, that he was doomed. The crocodile could swim around in the water all day, while he could only hold on for another minute or two . . . and even that seemed unthinkable. It was all over: he might as well just let go and drop into the jaws of the beast.

Then it happened.

A cry exploded from somewhere beyond and below the corridor: a booming, screaming wail that grew to such a pitch that it almost felt as though the entire tunnel was shaking. The wail turned into a deafening roar and, if anything, grew louder still. All at once, it ceased . . . and a dreadful silence took its place.

Decimus looked down, but the waters were still. The crocodile was nowhere to be seen.

The temptation was to let himself fall, but he couldn't bring himself to release his grip on the ceiling crevice. The crocodile could still be down there somewhere, swimming in the depths of the—

A weak splash from the mouth of the tunnel suddenly shook him from his reverie, and his gaze found the bank he'd originally squelched down in order to enter the water. The crocodile was emerging from the depths of the underground river. It scrambled on to the bank, moving far quicker than Decimus would have expected it to, and disappeared up the tunnel, heading towards the cave he'd originally dropped into. The noise must have spooked it; either that or the cry really had shaken the foundations of the catacombs and the reptile had reacted to the tremors by fleeing. Either way, the result was positive for Decimus.

He finally loosened his hold on the tunnel crevice and splashed into the water, swimming for the opposite end of the flooded passage with all his might. His arms ploughed through the murky river like spinning knives, and his legs kicked against the water with such force that he barely noticed the walls of the tunnel flying past him. Eventually, he emerged, coughing and spluttering, from the filthy water. Despite

slipping several times in the mud, he
managed to drag his exhausted body to the
edge of an ancient-looking flight of stone
steps . . . where he paused to catch his breath.

Lying still in the shadows, Decimus
suddenly remembered the glow that he'd
seen from the middle of the tunnel. He sat up
sharply, and turned to face the archway at the
top of the steps. The illumination was

definitely coming from the chamber beyond the stone flight, and it was a strangely distorted light that seemed to change from orange to green every few seconds before settling on a glow that was somewhere between the two colours.

Decimus hauled himself to his feet and, balling his hands into fists, began to ascend the stairs.

CHAPTER V

THE CAGES

The chamber beyond was very different to the gloomy tunnel he'd swum through in order to reach it. The strange light that had given the room its glow seemed to be coming from a fallen torch. Decimus noticed that it lay in the middle of the room as if dropped by a wanderer like himself, yet it was still burning brightly. There was one big difference between this torch and the torch he'd brought in, however: the flames were burning green, not orange. The rest of the room was in shadow.

Decimus crept over to the fallen torch and, very gingerly, lifted it from the ground. As he raised the flame up, a thick green liquid dripped from the end and pooled on the

floor. Decimus turned the torch over in his hands, watching as more of the sticky mixture dripped around him.

He wondered if the green liquid was somehow making the torch burn for longer, but the thoughts soon evaporated when the rest of the room was revealed by the light from the flames.

Decimus saw that there were two cages in the room, both connected to the ceiling by a series of chains. Inside each cage were row upon row of needle-thin spikes, and Decimus saw that these started at the top of the cages and tapered down so that the spikes almost – but not quite – reached the floor. He also noticed that the floors of the cages were missing, making both into the sort of traps that would not just maim but totally skewer the unfortunate souls who happened to wander beneath them. The chains must have been triggered by something or someone walking through . . .

It was then that Decimus saw Olu. At first, he'd taken a quick glance at both cages but had moved closer to the one on the left in

order to study it. Now, stepping over to the
opposite cage, he saw that his friend lay flat
on the floor, beneath the vicious bed of
spikes.

He was dead, no question.

Decimus gritted his teeth, and felt his eyes well up with tears. He thought of all the things he'd been through with Olu, the escape from Doom's arena and the journey on the slave ship. Now, he would never get a chance to say goodbye to his friend.

Overcome with sadness, Decimus dropped the torch and slumped on to the floor, trying to keep his sobs as quiet as possible in case they awoke the thing that had spooked the crocodile with its deafening scream.

He still had a hand to his face when, out of the corner of one eye, he saw Olu move his head.

'Mff,' the slave boy managed, his lips rubbing together so slightly that the movement was almost imperceptible.

'Olu!' Decimus rolled on to his belly and dragged himself closer to where his friend lay. From this new position, he could see that the spikes hadn't gone all the way into Olu's back. The boy was so thin – he'd always looked half starved to Decimus – that they hadn't penetrated much beyond the surface of his skin. Still, the pain must have been . . .

'I know what you're thinking,' said Olu, in a cracked voice.

Decimus managed a weakened smile. 'Yeah?' he said. 'What's that?'

'The same thing I thought when this happened to me: if I was Gladius, I'd be dead.'

Decimus thought of Gladius who was so

much bigger than Olu, and had to stop himself from laughing out loud.

'I'm going to get you out,' he said, eventually, leaping to his feet.

Olu groaned, but said nothing more.

'Let me see, here . . .'

Decimus looked at the chain that sprouted from the roof of the cage, and followed it with his eyes. The chain seemed to run through a hole in the ceiling, but it also emerged from a second hole near the chamber entrance.

Decimus left the torch beside the cage and hurried over to the root of the chain. Taking the thick links in both hands, he paused for a second in order to think.

If I don't get the cage off Olu in one go, if I

can't muster the strength and it slips . . .
I might end up killing him myself.

Decimus looked from the cage to the
chain, and back again. Then he took the links
in his hands once more. When he started to
heave on the chain, he
immediately put one, then
two feet against the
chamber wall. The cage was

unspeakably heavy, but Decimus pulled with such dogged determination that the weight seemed immaterial. The chain moved slowly, link by link. After a few seconds, Decimus was horizontal, his body forming a straight line as his feet pushed flat against the wall.

The cage rose up, and Olu half-scrambled, half-rolled out from beneath it. His back was a patchwork of bloody pinpricks.

Decimus let go of the chain and fell to the floor with a dull thud, puffing out a lungful of air. His arms flopped to his sides, and his legs twitched with the sudden release of the pressure.

'How?' he gasped, trying but failing to keep his voice low. 'How did you get in there?'

Olu turned to him, an agonized expression settling on his face.

'Having one of those fall on you is pretty easy,' he spat. 'Having one of those fall on you and survive, now that's hard.'

Decimus looked back at the cage full of spikes, and his lips split into a wide grin.

'I'm listening,' he said.

CHAPTER VI

FLOWERS

Olu tiptoed around the chamber as if he was certain another cage could drop at any moment. Arriving beside Decimus, he put a scarred finger to his lips.

'We have to be quiet,' he whispered. 'There's something else in these tunnels, something really big and really bad.'

'I know,' said Decimus, with a grave nod. 'I heard the bellow when I was swimming through the tunnel on the other side of that archway.'

Olu looked up.

'So you saw the crocodile?' he ventured.

'Yes; it nearly ripped me in half. How did you end up here?'

The thin slave sighed.

'Ruma and I were sent in together. The crocodile must have been in one of the other passages when we found the flooded corridor, because it seemed to come from nowhere. One second we were on the bank, the next it was crawling down the tunnel after us. We dived in and swam like a pair of lunatics. That's when we found this place.'

Decimus moved around behind Olu and checked his back for any deep wounds, but fortunately the damage seemed very superficial.

'Ruma saw the burning torch and went over to look at it, but before he reached the middle of the room I spotted that plate just inside the arch.'

Decimus suddenly lowered the torch and

squinted at the floor beside the entrance:
sure enough, there was a circular pad, half-
concealed by sand, set into the ground.

'I didn't see it!' he admitted.

'No,' said Olu. 'Neither did Ruma. I tried
to warn him. In fact, I ran to push him out of
the way, thinking that he was about to be
covered in arrows or something. That's when

I tripped and fell flat on my face. The cages came crashing down, and I was pinned inside. Ruma didn't have a clue what was happening until it was too late.'

'Didn't he try to get you out?'

'Of course, but he just didn't have the strength. Ruma is one of the toughest people I've ever met, but his arms are all bone and no muscle! He went off for help, instead.'

Decimus frowned at his skinny friend.

'Help? In this place?'

'Yeah; it was a slim chance, I know . . . but we knew Argon and Gladius were somewhere ahead of us. They were sent down first; the jailer to our cell told us that, but he didn't tell us when they went in.'

Decimus nodded.

'So they're all definitely down here?'

'They are,' muttered Olu, glaring around him. 'But I don't hold much hope for them. Ruma never came back, and that's not like him. If he was OK, he wouldn't have left me there; only the gods know how long I was lying under—'

'Shh! What's that?' Decimus was pointing at the only other exit to the chamber. 'There's something moving through there!'

He and Olu both crept across the room, making a point of checking for trap-plates as they went. When they reached the next chamber, however, Decimus soon realized that checking for traps would be practically impossible: the entire room was covered with thick green grass and a variety of brightly-coloured flowers.

'What the—' Olu stopped speaking and froze.

'I know,' said Decimus, raising the torch high above his head. 'This place is big.'

In truth, the new chamber was enormous.

As the light of the torch spread further and further, it revealed a vast cavern carpeted with all manner of beautiful and exotic-looking plants.

'Impossible,' Olu muttered, finally finding his voice.

'Mmm? What's that?'

'It's impossible! Look at this place! It was totally dark when we came in here: plants like this need light, how would they grow in such a room?'

'I don't know,' Decimus admitted. 'But I've never seen a torch that burns green, either . . . especially one that lights an entire room as if it were bathed in morning sunshine. I think it's the green liquid on the end; that's odd in itself. Come to think of it, this whole place feels very different. I'm not surprised Doom turned back at the beginning.'

Olu's eyes widened in surprise. 'He did?'

'Yeah; he showed me a map. It had about five corridors on it.'

Decimus allowed a few moments for his eyes to adjust to the field of flowers, then he began to move among them. Olu started to complain, but thought better of it and followed his friend instead, being extra careful to move as he moved and step where he stepped.

They were approximately halfway through the chamber when Decimus suddenly stopped dead. Saying nothing at first, he reached for Olu's arm and dragged him forward.

'You see that?' he whispered.

Olu strained to see into the dark corner Decimus was indicating.

'No,' he said, truthfully. 'I don't see anything except a bunch of blue flowers.'

'Right. Look past those, and to the left. You see anything now?'

Olu squinted at the area, and slowly nodded.

'There's someone lying there. Dead, d'you think?'

'No, definitely not. Can't you see the chest moving up and down? Wait here, and hold this high.'

Decimus passed the torch to Olu and began to creep through the long grass.

'Wait!' Olu whispered, urgently. 'It might

be an enemy. You don't know if—'

'Quiet!' snapped Decimus, reaching the prone figure and glancing back over his shoulder. 'It's Gladius . . . and he doesn't look very good.'

CHAPTER VII

THE MEADOW

Decimus crouched beside his best friend and placed a hand on his neck. Gladius was definitely alive, albeit in a deep, deep sleep.

Behind them, Olu approached with the torch, spilling more light on to the prone slave's face as he sat on the ground beside him.

'Gladius? Can you hear me?' Decimus took hold of his friend's shoulder and began, very gently, to shake him, but he got no response.

'He's out cold,' Olu observed. 'I can't believe I was trapped under the cage all that time and Gladius was just in the next room!'

'It's certainly strange,' muttered Decimus. 'Hmm ... didn't Ruma come this way after he left you?'

Olu nodded. 'He probably walked right past him, though. After all, I wouldn't have seen him if you hadn't pointed...'

Decimus was now shaking the big slave quite violently, but Gladius remained in a continued state of unconsciousness.

'He's not just asleep,' he said. 'He's breathing, but it's like he's enchanted or something.'

'Looking at him is making me feel tired,' Olu admitted, yawning loudly.

'Yeah, he looks so peaceful and—'
Decimus stopped talking mid-sentence, a faraway look in his eyes. Then he leapt to his feet and grabbed hold of Olu. 'Get up.'

'What? What's wrong with y—'

'It's the flowers. Move!'

Decimus practically dragged Olu off his feet in his dash to escape the grove: the skinny slave only just managed to hold on to the flaming torch.

When they reached the middle of the cavern, Decimus snatched the torch from Olu and held it aloft, shining a fresh wash of light over the area. He grimaced.

'The flowers put you to sleep,' he said.
'Gladius must have actually picked one or
something.'

'How do you know that?'

'Because I felt really tired when I was
crouching beside him, and you only started
to feel tired when you came over and sat
down. I tell you, this entire place is
CURSED.'

Olu shivered at the thought of the enchanted meadow, lying in wait for unprepared slaves, and his gaze returned to the sleeping form of Gladius.

'What are we going to do? We can't just leave him, can we?'

Decimus shook his head. 'Of course not. We're going to drag him out of here . . . but we're going to do it together, in one burst. With any luck, he'll wake up when he's away from here.'

'Why couldn't we have done that just then, rather than run away?'

Decimus pointed to the far exit.

'We still don't know what's beyond that arch,' he said. 'It's too dangerous to drag him blindly into another room. We already know there are crocodiles and only the gods know what else in that direction. We need to scout out the path ahead. Otherwise, we could walk from one kind of danger into another.'

Olu nodded, and the two friends turned their backs on the sleeping Gladius and began to approach the shadowy arch at the back of the cavern.

Unfortunately, they were in for a nasty surprise. Instead of the safe haven Decimus was hoping to find, the slaves found themselves on the edge of a giant rope bridge that spanned an immense chasm. The bridge itself was missing both planks and ropes in several places, and the whole thing looked about ready to collapse. The ledge on which they were standing was an odd shape, and tapered almost to a point before the posts supporting the bridge sprouted from it. There certainly wouldn't be much space to lay Gladius down if they managed to get him safely out of the enchanted cavern. In fact, Decimus was fairly certain that there wouldn't even be room for the three of them on the ledge if they were all standing.

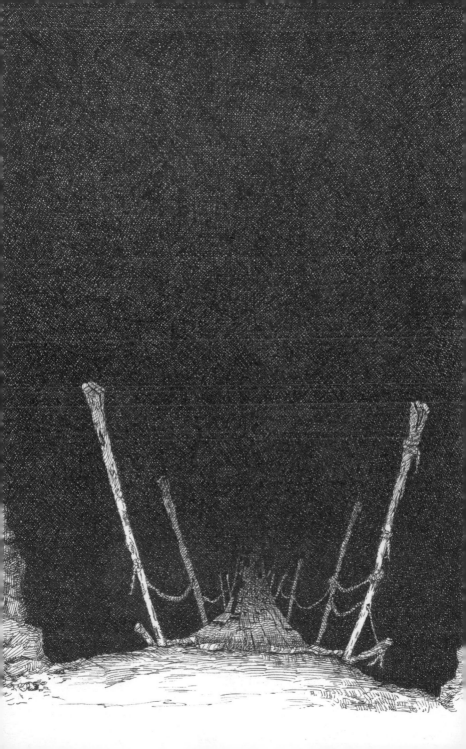

Still, at least there wasn't any immediate threat to concern them. Decimus voiced this thought to Olu, who shook his head and pointed skyward.

'Bats,' he said, squinting at the cavern roof. 'And big ones at that. There are hundreds of them.'

Decimus saw that his friend was right. The dark shapes were hanging overhead, so many that it looked as though a great black sheet had been nailed to the cavern roof. Every few seconds, one would make a tiny movement, which seemed to have an effect on all the others, causing the entire colony to shift slightly.

'We'll be OK as long as we don't disturb them,' he muttered, heading back to the meadow with the torch raised high above his head.

'You think?' said Olu, uneasily.

'Of course. They probably just want to be left alone.'

'Ha! Well, we certainly have no wish to disturb them, right? Besides, if that mammoth scream didn't wake them up . . .'

'It probably did: bats resettle quickly. We don't want to take any chances, though.'

Back in the underground meadow, Decimus turned to Olu with a serious expression on his face.

'We need to do this fast,' he said. 'Lifting Gladius isn't going to be easy, but the longer we're crouched beside those flowers, the more danger we're in. My guess is that if we breathe too much of their scent, we'll lose consciousness . . . and if that happens, it will be nearly impossible for whoever's left to get two others to the chasm. Agreed?'

Olu nodded. 'I'm ready if you are,' he said, crouching down and driving the torch into the grass until it stood upright.

'OK . . . deep breath?'

'Yes; here we go . . . on three . . .'

'One . . .'

'Two . . .'

'Three . . . go!'

Decimus and Olu took in two great

lungfuls of air, and made a frantic dash across the meadow.

They were halfway across the meadow when a roar shook the very foundations of the chamber . . .

COMING SOON

Decimus Rex is fighting his way through the perilous maze beneath the arena to locate the Blade of Fire, a legendary sword that Doom is intent upon possessing. But before he can retrieve the sword, Decimus must first rescue his friends. Will he manage it, or is his time about to run out?

THE BLADE OF FIRE

ARENA COMBAT

Get ready to challenge your friends! Each Gladiator Boy book will contain a different trial – collect them all to run your own Arena of Doom – either at home or in the school playground.

TRIAL 5
DEAD ENDS

In Gladiator Boy: Rescue Mission, Decimus has to negotiate his way through a deadly labyrinth. Now it's your turn! Only, this is a game of imagination and only the referee will be able to SEE the maze you're walking through!

GAME PROCEDURE

The referee player takes a good long look at the maze on the next spread.

The referee chooses which way up to hold the book (i.e. which entrance he wants the player to enter through). Then he puts a finger on the entrance and describes the choices to the first player. Example: 'OK, you're at the start of the maze. You can go ahead, left or right.'

The player then progresses through the maze, with the referee describing the choices each time (left, right, etc.).

Once the player has found his way out of the maze, the next player takes a turn.

The player who hit the LEAST dead ends before they got out is declared the winner.

This trial is played by taking on the character of a slave from Gladiator Boy. The profile in the following pages will add to your growing collection of characters! There are more in the other Gladiator Boy books!

CHARACTER PROFILE
GLADIUS

NAME: Gladius

FROM: Brindisium

HEIGHT: 1.65 metres

BODY TYPE: Heavy

BEST FRIEND: Decimus

CELLMATE: Decimus

GLADIUS QUIZ: How well do you know Gladius? Can you answer the following three questions?

1. WHAT IS IT THAT DECIMUS REX BELIEVES GLADIUS COULD HAVE FILLED IN BETTER THAN SLAVIOUS DOOM?

2. WHO GETS A HORRIBLE IMAGE OF GLADIUS IMPALED ON A SPIKE AS A WAKING NIGHTMARE?

3. 'IF I WAS GLADIUS, I'D BE DEAD.' WHO SAYS THIS LINE?

Answers: 1. Map, page 29 2. Decimus, page 46 3. Olu, page 71

WEAPON PROFILE MANACLES

Manacles might not be classed as a weapon in the usual sense, but they were certainly used against slaves throughout the world. Manacles are a device for clasping the hands. They consist of two wrist-sized metal rings connected by a chain. Occasionally, the connecting chain would be lightweight, but mostly it was very heavy, dragging the poor slaves to their knees and forcing them to stagger as they moved along.

Leg irons, pictured right, were also used to restrict the slaves' movement and iron collars were used to keep them in a chained line. Sometimes, the prisoners were even attached to a horse or cart and dragged along kicking and screaming as dust flew up in their faces.

GLADIATOR BOY

Check out the Gladiator Boy website for games, downloads, activities, sneak previews and lots of fun! You can even get extra pieces of the arena and fantastic action figures! Sign up to the newsletter to receive exclusive extra content and the opportunity to enter special competitions.

WWW.GLADIATORBOY.COM

LET BATTLE COMMENCE!

MAKE YOUR OWN ARENA OF DOOM

1. Carefully cut around the outline of the arena section. Ask an adult to help if necessary.
2. Fold across line A. Use a ruler to get a straight edge.
3. Fold across line B. Use a ruler to get a straight edge.
4. Ask an adult to help you score along lines C & D with a pair of sharp scissors.
5. Fold up over line E and push the window out.
6. Repeat instructions 1 to 5 for every Arena of Doom piece collected.
7. Glue the top of each tab and stick them to the next piece of the arena. Repeat as necessary.

CHECK OUT THE WEBSITE FOR A PHOTO OF THE COMPLETE ARENA.

TO MAKE YOUR ACTION FIGURE

1. Cut around the outline of the figure. Ask an adult to help if necessary.
2. Cut along slot X at the bottom of the figure.
3. Cut out Gladiator Boy rectangle.
4. Cut along slot Y.
5. Slot figure into slot Y.